PONY CAMP
diaries

Chloe and Cracker

D1439750

STRIPES PUBLISHING LTD
An imprint of the Little Tiger Group
1 Coda Studios, 189 Munster Road,
London SW6 6AW

A paperback original
First published in Great Britain by Stripes Publishing Ltd in 2007
This edition published in 2019

Text copyright © Kelly McKain 2007, 2019
Illustration © Mandy Stanley 2006, 2019

ISBN: 978-1-78895-019-0

PONY CAMP
diaries

Chloe and Cracker

by Kelly McKain

Illustrated by Mandy Stanley

stripes

To George, with love - thanks for all those
trips to Redwings Horse Sanctuary!

With special thanks to pony guru
Janet Rising, star instructor Jody Maile
and all at Ealing Riding School.

THIS DIARY BELONGS TO

Chloe

Dear Riders,

A warm welcome to Sunnyside Stables!

Sunnyside is our home and for the next week it will be yours too! We're a big family – my husband Johnny and I have two children, Millie and James, plus two dogs ... and all the ponies, of course!

We have friendly yard staff and a very talented instructor, Sally, to help you get the most out of your week. If you have any worries or questions about anything at all, just ask. We're here to help, and we want your holiday to be as enjoyable as possible – so don't be shy!

As you know, you will have a pony to look after as your own for the week. Your pony can't wait to meet you and start having fun! During your stay, you'll be caring for your pony, improving your riding, enjoying long country hacks, learning new skills and making friends.

And this week's special activity is a challenging treasure hunt. Just imagine you and your pony cantering across the countryside together, solving clues! Add swimming, games, films, barbecues and a gymkhana and you're in for a fun-filled holiday to remember!

This special Pony Camp Diary is for you to fill with all your holiday memories. We hope you'll write all about your adventures here at Sunnyside Stables – because we know you're going to have lots!

Wishing you a wonderful time with us!

Jody xx

Sunnyside Stables

hay barn

stables x 4

feed room

Barn

Stables x 4

ME on CRACKER

To upper fields →

Monday morning
– at Pony Camp!

Jody, the lady who runs Sunnyside Stables, gave
me this cool diary when I arrived just now. Her
letter at the front says it's to write down all the
adventures I have this week. It's fantastic here
– there are two outdoor manèges and lots of
cute ponies and dogs everywhere and even
a swimming pool! I'm hoping to have lots of
adventures – especially jumping ones!

I really wanted to come on this week because
when Mum rang up and spoke to Jody, she said
they're holding a special jumping competition on
the last day. In our lessons, we're going to work
on building up to an eight-jump course, and it's
even going to include some cross-country fences
for fun – I can't wait!

I love jumping but I've only done a couple
of smaller courses at clear round events at my

local riding school. I'm really hoping to improve
while I'm here – and I'm desperate to go clear
in Friday's competition.

The reasons I want a clear round so much
are:

a. because I've never had one
before so it will be a big challenge
for me and

b. to make Dad proud of me.

Although Dad knows how much I love ponies
(I'm always talking about getting my own one
day!), he's never actually seen me ride. He's
always working, even at weekends. But he said
he'll really, really try to come with Mum to pick
me up on Friday, then he'll be able to see me in
the jumping competition and I can amaze him
with my clear round (fingers crossed!). I really
hope he keeps his word and doesn't get stuck
at work as usual.

☾ Chloe and Cracker ☽

Jody

Sally

As soon as I got here, I kept asking Jody what we'll be doing every day because I was really excited. She smiled and said Sally, the instructor, will explain that when everyone arrives, but I really, really wanted to know straight away so she gave me a copy of the timetable to stick into my diary. She has warned me that it will change, though, because we have special activities on some days. Like, it says in her letter we're going on a treasure hunt this week – that sounds really fun!

Here's the timetable for the week:

Pony Camp Timetable

8am: Wake up, get dressed, have breakfast

8.45am: Help on the yard, bring in the ponies from field, muck out stables, do feeds, etc.

9.30am: Prepare ponies for morning lessons (quick groom, tack up, etc.)

10am: Morning riding lesson

11am: Morning break - drink and biscuits

11.20am: Pony Care lecture

12.30pm: Lunch and free time

2pm: Afternoon riding lesson

3pm: Break - drink and biscuits

3.20pm: Pony Care lecture

4.30pm: Jobs around the yard (i.e. cleaning tack, sweeping up, mixing evening feeds, turning out ponies)

5.30pm: Free time before dinner

6pm: Dinner (and clearing up!)

7pm: Evening activity

8.30pm: Showers and hot chocolate

9.30pm: Lights out and NO TALKING!

Wow! There's so much to do here! I just can't wait to find out which pony I'm getting – having my own pony to look after for a whole week will be fab!

This morning we're having an assessment lesson where we all ride in together, and then Sally will decide who goes in which group. So the timetable's different already because there's no lecture this morning. It's now 10.35am and not everyone is here yet, including the girls who are sharing my room – but, oh, now I can hear talking and clumping on the stairs. Maybe it's them!

Two minutes later

It *was* them!

The two girls I'm sharing with have gone downstairs to help on the yard — we are all still waiting for a couple of others to arrive, but the adults keep telling each other that there's a hold-up on the M3 so we're running a bit later than planned.

I'm going down in a minute but first I just wanted to do a quick profile of my room-mates for my diary.

Name: Isabella

Age: 12

Lives: Buckinghamshire, which is sort of near to London but still in the countryside.

Description: Quite tall for 12, goes to a school for

girls only, has amazing green eyes and long wavy
brown hair and plays the cello and has packed
three different swimsuits because she couldn't
decide which to bring (I've only got one!).
She says her friends call her Bella, and we
can too (how cool!).

Name: Georgia

Age: 12

Lives: Georgia comes all
the way from Devon, which I
suppose isn't actually far from
here, but it's a long way from
where I live (i.e. London).

Description: Short blondish
hair. She seems very sensible and mature
for 12, but she's also really friendly so that's
okay. She has two younger brothers and one
younger sister and says she has to help her
mum and dad look after them quite a lot.

The best thing is that Isabella and Georgia are both really into jumping too and they also chose this week specially to come to Sunnyside, so they could spend lots of time focusing on it. Also, they're both really nice and are not leaving me out just because I'm a weeny bit younger than them, which older girls can sometimes do.

Oh, I have to go – Bella's calling me down to the yard. Maybe it's time to find out which ponies we're getting. I'm so excited just thinking about it! Fingers crossed mine's a good jumper!

Still Monday morning,
in our break

I am quickly writing this because I've got something exciting to put down that can't wait till later. The girls who were delayed are here now and we're just about to have our assessment lesson. But even though we haven't been given our ponies yet I have already met the perfect one for me.

What happened was, when I got outside, Jody explained that while we were waiting for the last two girls to arrive, we could get on with some yard work. She gave me mucking-out duty with this really nice stable girl called Lydia. That's when I met Charm, who is an amazingly gorgeous grey Connemara. I fell

in love with him straight away and Lydia said I could lead him out and tie him up in the yard while we did his stable. I gave him a big stroke and pat on the way and he whinnied and nuzzled into my T-shirt.

Lydia

While we were working I asked Lydia about him and she told me what a great jumper he is. That just made me want him to be my pony even more!

When Lydia and I had put the new straw down on top of the clean bits of bedding and spread it all out, I got to lead Charm back in, and I whispered to him that I really hoped he'd be my pony for the week. After a while, the other girls arrived and Jody called us all back into the main yard and introduced us to each other and the Sunnyside Stables team.

As well as me and Bella and Georgia there is Millie, Jody's daughter, who I read about in the welcome letter. The girls sharing her room are called Suki and Mai and they go to an international school in London. They are both eight and three-quarters and are actually from Japan.

Suki   Mai

Then there are the little ones, Olivia, Asha and Joelle (who is only just seven and the youngest of all), and they're in a room together.

Olivia   Asha   Joelle

Me, Bella and Georgia are all really excited about the jumping and we're crossing our fingers that we get put in the group to do it. Bella and Georgia have jumped a bit but neither of them have done a competition yet, so I've probably got the most experience, even though it's not much.

I really, really hope I've got Charm. I've worked out I've got a 33.3333333333% chance of getting him — he's a bit big for the younger girls and Millie has her own pony, of course, and so I reckon it will be between me, Georgia and Bella.

Still Monday,
after the ponies were given out

Well, it didn't exactly go as I'd hoped, but I'm
trying not to be too disappointed. We were
all waiting in the yard with our hats and body
protectors and everything, and Sally was reading
from a list while Lydia brought the ponies
out, one by one. They were already tacked up,
because some of the girls had been helping do
that while I was mucking out.

I was really excited and as Lydia led Charm
out I had all my fingers crossed for luck, but
then Sally said, "Isabella, you're on Charm.
I hope you two will hit it off. Charm's a superb
jumper and he has lovely manners." Well, my
heart sank and I had to blink fast to stop tears
coming into my eyes. Bella looked so excited
and I forced myself to smile at her.

Bella thanked Sally and stroked Charm's nose

before leading him over to the mounting block.
As he nudged her shoulder happily, I couldn't
help thinking that he should have been nudging
my shoulder instead.

Then Sally said, "Chloe, you've got Cracker.
He's a really spirited, cheeky little thing so you'll
need all your experience!" She didn't mention
his great jumping or good manners, but he is
quite sweet, I suppose – a grey Welsh Section
B, with big eyes and a cute pink bit on his nose.
Lydia says he's 12.2hh and I feel a bit big for
him – my heels are almost off his sides. Charm's
over a hand higher. I just wish ... but there's
no point in wishing. I haven't got Charm
so I'll just have to try and make the best
of it. I don't want to waste my holiday
moping!

I'll write about the assessment lesson in a
minute, but first here's my drawing of who got
which pony:

Chloe and Cracker

Bella - Charm
- my fave!

Mai - Star

Georgia - Prince,
a really sweet cobby
piebald

Olivia - Ebony

Me - Cracker

Joelle - Monsoon

Asha - Sugar

Suki - Twinkle

Millie is riding her pony
Tally, of course.

We had the assessment lesson and it went okay. Millie didn't ride with us – Jody said she had to get on with her holiday homework instead. Poor thing!

At first we just had to walk and trot and think about our position and making good transitions. Then we did some turns and circles and changes of rein, and at the end we all had a canter to the back of the ride, except Joelle 'cos she hasn't done much riding and she only knows walk and trot at the moment. Instead, she turned Monsoon into the middle and Sally held on to her while we cantered on one rein and then the other.

Sally was right about Cracker, he is quite cheeky. I really had to keep my inside leg on all the way round or he'd fall in off the track, and when I just gently used my legs to get him listening (he wasn't going into trot for anyone!) he did a couple of little bucks. I didn't really mind, but I tried not to look at Bella trotting round perfectly on Charm, or at their lovely effortless transitions, which didn't involve any kicking or flailing arms like mine did.

Afterwards we put our ponies back in the stables (or in pens in the big barn for the ones who live out) and untacked. I gave Cracker a brush down and made sure he had enough water. Then we came back into the yard and gathered round Sally to hear the news.

Here are the groups we're in:

Group A: Suki, Mai, Olivia, Joelle, Asha.

Group B: Me, Bella, Georgia, Millie

Our group will be doing the jumping and entering the clear round comp at the end of the week! Group A is the less experienced group, and on Friday they're going to do gymkhana games instead of jumping the course. Sally told them they'll still get to have a go at jumping in their lessons so they won't be missing out.

When we heard that we
were doing the jumping
comp, Bella grabbed me
and Georgia and we all
leaped up and down in a
huggy group. I was excited

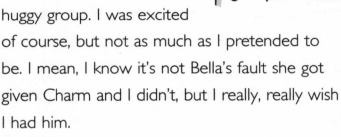

of course, but not as much as I pretended to
be. I mean, I know it's not Bella's fault she got
given Charm and I didn't, but I really, really wish
I had him.

I thought I would've forgotten about Charm
by now — but I just can't seem to. I'll have to
make sure I hide how I feel. I don't want to fall
out with my new friends when I've only just met
them! Maybe things will be better after the first
jumping lesson, when we've made a start and
I'm on my way to getting that clear round. Now
I've got a handle on Cracker's bad habits I'll be a
whole lot stricter!

Monday 6.32pm
In our room

We're going swimming tonight for our evening
activity, but Jody says we have to let our tea go
down for half an hour first. We're all squashed
on to the top bunk, which is Georgia's (Bella
is below and I am in the single bed by the
window), writing in our diaries. We were up
here talking before but Bella kept
going on and on about how
amazing Charm is, and it was
really getting on my nerves,
so I suggested we did some
writing instead.

    This afternoon it was really
scorching hot so Sally said we'd have our Pony
Care lecture first and then have our riding
lesson afterwards when it was cooler. She
showed us how to tie the ponies up correctly

and where all the equipment goes so we don't leave anything lying about that could be a danger, and what to wear and everything.

Then after the break we had our first jumping lesson. I was so excited! We had a warm-up for about twenty minutes, working in all the paces on each rein. When we stopped to put our stirrups up a couple of holes, Georgia got worried that Sally was going to start setting up the course right away. But Sally explained that we'll be starting with trotting poles and singles and then building up gradually, so Georgia felt okay after that.

We did some basic pole work, then we practised trotting on and going into the jumping position down the long side, which was quite tricky. Cracker enjoyed it because I didn't exactly have all my powers of steering in that position and so he got to cut the corner off and wander across the manège!

Then Sally set up a simple cross pole. First
we approached in trot (except Millie, because
Tally just charged at it in canter!). After a couple
of goes we came up in trot and then cantered
away, and we had to keep the canter till we
reached the back of the ride. Cracker cut the
corner off the first time, but after that I got my
inside leg on straight after the jump so he had
to behave. There's so much to think about with
him on just one jump, I have no idea how I'm
going to get round a whole course!

Then we cantered the whole thing and he
cut the corner off again before I even had time
to think. I got a bit annoyed with him and felt
like giving up. It must have showed because Sally
called out, "He's perfectly capable, Chloe, he's
just seeing what he can get away with. Circle
him round and go again." Then when I went
over the next time, she shouted "Inside leg on!"
as soon as I hit the ground. At least I kept him

on the track down the short side, although I bet
I looked really clumsy and unseated.

I've just moved over a bit to make sure
Bella can't see what I'm writing. I feel really bad
even putting this down, but I have to because
it's what happened. We finished off the lesson
by working over a double, and Sally made the
second pole into an upright. Cracker did okay,
but he only just cleared it, whereas Charm
sailed miles over and I felt really
jealous again. I bet Bella
will go clear in the comp
without even trying and
she's probably not even
that bothered whether
she does or not! I bet
her dad makes a big fuss of
her whatever she does. It just doesn't seem fair
that I really need Charm to impress my dad and
she's got him.

Oh, I feel awful and I wish I hadn't put that now. It's not Bella's fault she got Charm. I hate feeling this way – it's just not like me at all. Right, I'm going to climb down from here right this second and hide this diary somewhere in my stuff.

And then I'm going to try my hardest to forget all about Charm.

Tuesday lunchtime

We've just had lunch and I'm sitting outside on the benches in the sun.

I was going to write in here when we went to bed last night (I've got a cool little torch on my key ring) but after two lots of riding, then swimming as well, I'd run out of energy. Still, even though we were all tired, we kept bursting into giggles after lights out because Bella was whispering this story to us about a boy down her road who keeps asking her out. Georgia and Bella are brilliant fun — I'm so glad I'm sharing a room with them!

This morning we had our Pony Care lecture on tack and tacking up. I knew some of it already, but it was really good to learn about all the different bits. Also, Lydia was doing the lecture and she demonstrated tacking up on Suki's lovely yellow dun Twinkle and then she

undid it all and told us to bring Charm and
Sugar out too. So we practised tacking up on
them in threes, which was cool 'cos I got to
spend time hanging around with Charm and
making a fuss of him without it seeming strange.

In our lesson this morning we did flat work,
and Sally explained that it will help us with our
jumping. Apparently the three important things
you need to jump well are balance, impulsion
and rhythm. I wanted to call out, "And you need
a good pony who listens to you and picks his
feet up!". But I didn't dare say that because Sally
is quite strict most of the time and I thought she
might get annoyed.

So we did all these turns and circles, and
some riding straight down the centre and
three-quarter lines, and we worked on making
lots of transitions, which Sally says is good for
impulsion. Then we started practising figures of
eight, dropping into trot and changing our canter

lead in the middle – we'll need to do that twice when we jump the course. At first Cracker just wanted to carry on up the track and not come through the middle at all. Then when I finally got him to trot through the diagonal he refused to go back into canter, so in frustration I kicked him with my heels.

"Get yourself together and focus, Chloe!" Sally called out. "You can't just sit there and then blame Cracker when he doesn't canter!"

me v. flustered !

I felt really red and flustered when she said that – I wasn't just sitting there. Bella always got her canter back as soon as she asked – and on the right leg too. Oh, it's just so annoying! Sally probably thinks I'm completely rubbish – if I was on Charm she'd see that I really *can* ride, and that I *do* put my outside leg back and everything – it's not my fault that Cracker doesn't listen to me!

I was so frustrated I made things a bit
awkward in the yard after the lesson, although
I didn't mean to. Bella and I had tied up our
ponies next to each other to untack and give
them a brush down. The ponies have their
own grooming kits and each bit of the kit has
the pony's name on. Well, somehow Charm's
body brush had gone missing and she
asked me if she could borrow
Cracker's. I was about to
say yes, but somehow a
big "No!" came out of my
mouth.

"But you're not even using it," said Georgia,
looking confused.

I felt myself going all red and flushed again,
like I did when Sally kept correcting me in the
lesson. "But I'm just about to," I mumbled.

I wished I hadn't said no, but I didn't know
how to get out of it, so I picked up the brush,

planning to use it quickly then give it straight to Bella. But by that time Georgia had stepped in and lent hers, and it looked like I'd started using mine just to be awkward. Urgh!

Luckily they forgot about it over lunch and everything was fine by the time we got our fruit and yoghurt, but I can't let Bella find out how I feel about Charm – I'll have to try even harder to get over my jealousy.

♡ Chloe and Cracker ♡

Tuesday, in my room after a lovely tea of jacket potatoes with tuna and sweetcorn - yum!

Tonight we're having a table tennis tournament in the games room, and we've only got twenty mins before it starts so I'm going to have to write really fast! I'm alone up here 'cos Bella and Georgia are on washing-up duty.

Before we got our ponies out to mount up for our jumping lesson, Sally called us into the manège. The course had been set up! There were four fences completely up and four trotting poles to mark where the other ones would be. We all walked round the route and Sally explained the best approach to take for each jump and where the tricky bits might be. This is what the whole course is going to look like:

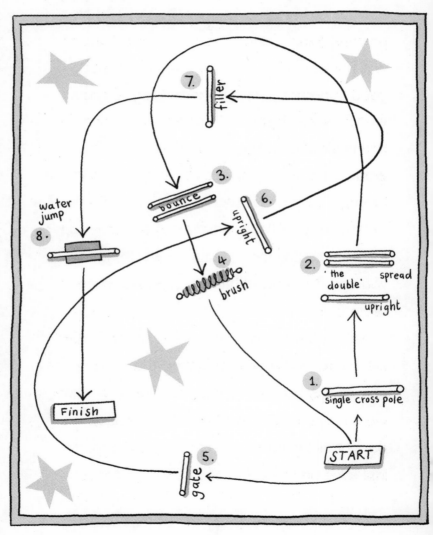

This afternoon the only fences up were the single and spread at the start and then the bounce and brush in the middle. We had to practise going round the trotting pole (which was marking where the filler will be) to get a good approach to the bounce. I can see now why Sally was being so strict about me not letting Cracker cut the corner off in the flat work. It's a tricky turn and I'll need every inch I can get to line him up properly over these middle jumps. The thing is, you really have to hit the bounce properly because if you're too long you'll end up knocking the second bit of the fence down.

Sally said me and Millie were both still cutting the corner and she put a block there for us to go round. Tally got the message quickly, but Cracker went inside it twice and Sally made me keep doing it till I got it right. By then I had so much inside leg on I thought my calf might explode!

After ages of trying, me and Cracker finally got over the brush and back to trot in time to change canter lead (on to the correct leg at last!). We made it round the corner and over the centre of the trotting pole that marked where the gate would be.

"Honestly, Cracker," I said, as we all walked round on a long rein to let our ponies cool down, "why couldn't you just get it right in the first place? We've got so much to do before the comp — and I've had to spend an hour teaching you not to cut a corner. You're such a pest!"

"Oh, Chloe, he's not," I heard someone say.

I looked up and was really embarrassed to find that Sally had heard me telling Cracker off. I went red and tried to explain. "It's just, my dad's coming on Friday and I've promised him I'll get a clear round, but Cracker won't listen to me round the corners and I'm sure he's going to knock the gate and I don't know how I'll get him

back into trot in time after the brush to change
canter lead and…"

I trailed off. Sally looked
annoyed. "Chloe, honestly!" she
cried. "Poor Cracker's doing his
best! You need to work
on the communication
between you, and to be firmer
when you ask for something.
If you looked up and ahead
more round the tight corner he'd understand
what you wanted better. It's true he's not a very
experienced jumper, but he tries hard and he's
getting there."

"I know, but it doesn't seem fair that I have
to work so hard when *some of the other ponies*
just get it right first time and…" I began, but
Sally cut me off.

We both knew who I meant by some of the
other ponies.

Sally
CROSS !

"But you're not on the other ponies," she said firmly. "I gave Cracker to you because I thought you could bring out the best in him. I still think you can, Chloe, but you need to work together as a team and build up a partnership, like Bella has with Charm."

That really stung me.

"Just be careful that you're not so desperate to achieve a clear round in the competition that you actually stop yourself from doing it," Sally said then.

As she gave Cracker a pat and walked off I stared after her. Even thinking about it now, I still don't understand what she meant. How can I stop myself from getting something by really wanting it? That doesn't make sense.

Oh, Millie's just come up to say the table tennis tournament's about to start.

 I'd better go!

◡ Chloe and Cracker ◡

Tuesday night

When we got into our beds, Bella was going on and on about how great Charm is so I pretended to fall asleep, and after a while she and Georgia fell asleep too, so now I can write in here by the light of my key-ring torch.

While Bella and Georgia were playing against each other in the table tennis tournament I slipped off to the yard to visit Charm. I spent ages leaning over his stable door, stroking him and telling him how much I wish he was my pony.

I felt a bit bad then, because Cracker hadn't been turned out yet, and I could see him in the barn, munching hay. I'm sure he saw me too – but I didn't go over and fuss him. I would have, if I'd had more time. Maybe. But I didn't really feel like it.

The table tennis was fun – Millie's older brother James organized it with their dad. Millie actually won, but she said the second-place person should get the prize, 'cos she's here all the time and she plays a lot. So Mai won the *Spirit* DVD – when she gets back to school she's going to ask her house mistress to put it on for all the girls. She and Suki board at their school because their parents are in Japan. They must be used to not seeing their mums and dads much because they don't seem to miss them at all.

I'm not used to it though, and after I got knocked out of the table tennis tournament I was suddenly desperate to speak to Mum, so

Jody let me phone. Dad answered, as he'd just got in the door from work. The good news is that he's almost definitely coming to the gymkhana on Friday. The bad news is that he said, "So, still reckon you're on for that clear round you promised me?"

I said, "Definitely!" but my stomach was churning. Then Mum came on the phone and I told her all the good bits of what we'd been doing this week and none of the awkward things like how jealous I feel about Bella getting Charm. I don't want her to worry that I'm not settling in here.

Anyway, I have to think positively about that clear round. There are still three days to sort out my jumping before the comp — I'll make more effort with Cracker tomorrow and hopefully everything will go well!

Wednesday, after tea

I haven't had time to write in here all day, but loads of things have happened. Our flat work lesson this morning went fine and the Pony Care lectures on feeding and points of the horse and everything were really fun. But this afternoon's jumping lesson was a disaster.

Everything has gone wrong. I mean, *really* wrong. I've fallen out with Bella and Georgia. And the worst thing of all is that it's my own stupid fault.

This afternoon when we rode into the manège all eight jumps were in place, and my stomach flipped with excitement. Before starting at the beginning, though, we did some work on the last jump, which is the water tray.

Sally explained that although it's only a single it's the most challenging fence, because ponies can find the water a bit spooky. She said we'd

just walk our ponies through the water first,
without the pole, so they could get used to it.

Well, Charm didn't mind at all and Tally
splashed straight through it. Even Prince was fine
once he'd had a good look.

But not Cracker.

He walked through it on the second try,
and for a moment I thought we'd be okay. But
when Sally put the pole up, even at a much
lower height than it will be on Friday, he just
absolutely refused to go over, even in trot. He
had this way of seeming like he was going over,
then scampering sideways at the last minute,

and it caught me out every time. After a few
tries, I felt like I was holding everyone up, and I
had to do the fast-blinking thing to keep myself
from crying. Sally came over and explained that
Cracker was finding it easier to run out because
the fence is narrower. She said, "You just have
to ride forward positively and look ahead to the
finish. You're looking down at the water, and
that's going to make him think it's scarier than
it is."

I wanted to say that I was doing my best, but
I didn't dare. I tried looking ahead and riding
Cracker forward like Sally said, but it still didn't
work. Then I got annoyed and rode him at it
quite fast, and this time when he lurched to the
left I came flying off on to the woodchips.

Everyone laughed. I realize now they only
meant it in a friendly way but I didn't see it like
that at the time. As I got up and dusted myself
down I didn't look anyone in the eye. I got on

again and trotted to the back of the ride, but what I really wanted to do was run indoors, get in bed and have a good cry with my head under the covers. I'd thought we'd only have to worry about the gate when it came to getting a clear round, but then I realized we had to deal with the water jump as well and the whole thing just seemed hopeless. It didn't help that Charm was flying over everything without even trying and Sally kept saying, "Well ridden, Bella!".

Then things got even worse. When we tried the last couple of jumps together, I still couldn't get over the water tray. Bella offered to give me a lead so Cracker could follow Charm over, which made me feel absolutely stupid, like she was just showing off and trying to make me look silly. "No thanks, I'm fine," I mumbled, without looking at her. I know now that she wasn't being mean at all, but it's too late to take back what happened.

Anyway, Sally said it was nearly time to finish and let us all have a pop over a single, to end on a positive note. I didn't feel positive though, and as we walked our ponies round on a long rein to cool them off, I was simmering with fury at Bella.

As I dismounted on the yard, I found her right behind me and when I saw her happy, smiling face I just snapped. "You were only

offering me a lead to make me look hopeless!" I hissed. "You think you're such a good rider, but it's only 'cos Charm's so good that he makes you look good too. It's not fair that you get the easy-peasy pony while I'm stuck with Cracker!"

And then I marched Cracker straight through to the barn and untacked on my own, not even waiting to hear if Bella said anything back.

I got on with brushing him down, but my
heart was pounding and I felt terrible — how
could I have said something so mean? Everything
had gone wrong and I wanted to ring Mum and
get her to drive down here and take me home.

That was when Olivia and Asha came
up, looking nervous. "Bella's crying," Asha
announced.

I felt like running away, but I made myself
follow them back to the main yard.

When I got over to Charm's
stable, Georgia had her arm
round Bella, and Suki, Mai and
Joelle were hovering beside
them, looking worried.

But before I could say anything Georgia
looked up and gave me a glare so cold it made
me shiver. "How could you be so mean to Bella
when she was only offering you a lead to help
you?" she hissed.

The younger girls all stared at me and I felt completely awful, like I wanted the ground to open up and swallow me. I realized that there was only one way to explain how I'd acted – I had to tell the truth. I took a deep breath. "Bella, I'm sorry," I began. Georgia snorted but I clenched my fists and carried on.

"The thing is, I wanted Charm," I admitted. "I've been trying not to let it show, but when I was struggling so much on Cracker, I couldn't help thinking, if I only had Charm... I didn't want to feel jealous and I tried my best to hide it–"

But Georgia interrupted me. "It's even worse that you've pretended to be her friend all this time!" she said icily.

"But I am her friend!" I cried. I tried to get Bella to look at me but I only caught a glimpse of her red, tear-stained face before she buried it in Georgia's fleece again.

"It's okay, Bella, you've got real friends, forget about her," said Georgia. "Come on, you'll be okay with us lot." And with that she led Bella off towards the farm house. The others followed, giving me very cross looks. I started crying then and hurried back into the house. I tried to creep through the kitchen to get upstairs but Jody was at the sink, testing Millie on her times tables. As soon as she saw my face she made me sit down and tell her what had happened. While I was explaining it all, and trying to stop crying, I realized that I've been so focused on Charm I haven't even given Cracker a chance. I felt like I'd been mean to him, as well as Bella, and that made me cry even more.

I don't blame Georgia for being so angry either. She must think I'm such a horrible person after today. "I said sorry," I sniffled, "but I don't think Bella will want to be friends with me any more."

Millie got me some Jaffa Cakes even though it was nearly time for tea and Jody gave me a hug, saying, "I'm sure deep down Bella knows you didn't mean it. You can always try apologizing again later. Just give her time to calm down and it'll blow over, you'll see. Now how about helping me get the tea going?"

So I did, and then I set the table.

I dreaded having to face the girls at tea, but Millie sat next to me and no one said anything nasty. I tried to smile at Bella a couple of times but she still wouldn't look at me. I didn't dare smile at Georgia in case she did her icy glare and it made me start crying again.

It's so lucky my washing-up duty tonight was with Millie. After we'd cleared up, she had to carry on with her maths practice, so when I'd put everything away I just sat down next to

her and got my Pony Camp Diary out and I've
been writing in here ever since. I should have
gone to the games room for the film, but I sort
of haven't quite made it yet. There's someone
else I need to say sorry to (as well as Bella), and
it can't wait till tomorrow, or even one more
minute.

I just went to ask Jody and she says I can go
up to the field because Lydia's there, but I have
to come back when she does. And Jody's given
me a carrot from the fridge.

Got to go now!

Wednesday, after lights out

I'm in bed, writing by the light of my key-ring torch again. I tried to hang around in Millie's room for as long as possible after lights out, hiding under the covers at the bottom of her bed, but when Jody came up to check on us all she made me come back in here. Luckily Bella and Georgia were asleep so I didn't have to face them.

At least me and Cracker are friends now. Luckily he came when I called him over. I leaned over the fence, gave him a big pat and said sorry for being so mean, and especially for spending time with Charm when I could have been with him. I ruffled his mane and whispered, "Cracker, I'm so sorry for blaming you for our bad jumping when I should have been thinking of us as a team and connecting with you better and riding you more positively."

Cracker looked at me with his big black
eyes and I'm sure he understood. I added, "I've
brought you a carrot to say sorry." When I held
it out he munched it right up, so I know it's all
okay between us now.

I wish I could just give Bella
a carrot and then she'd like
me again. I've just thought,
maybe I should be calling
her Isabella now because she is only Bella to her
friends and maybe I'm not her friend any more.
Urgh! I hope Jody's right and that things will
blow over tomorrow.

Goodnight!

Thursday 11.12am, before the treasure hunt

We're just having some drinks and biscuits before we go out on the treasure hunt. My timetable from Jody has changed again today because we had our lecture first instead of the lesson. Sally said we'd need the skills for going on the treasure hunt.

I thought that meant the lecture would be on solving clues, but actually it was about road safety and first aid, and how to put boots and bandages on your pony and what to do if you get lost in the countryside. I've bandaged Cracker's legs because Sally said we might be going through the woods, and we have to be as prepared as possible. We also put our ponies' bridles on over their head collars, and each clipped a lead rope on to our D-rings so that we could dismount and have a picnic without the ponies galloping off. When I'd finished all the preparation, I made a big fuss of Cracker and told him how smart he looked.

I have sort of smiled at Isabella a couple of times and Georgia hasn't made a horrible face at me or anything so that's a bit better at least. The other girls seem to have forgotten about our falling-out because when I helped Asha to do Sugar's bandages and Olivia to put on Ebony's boots they were both chattering away to me as if nothing had happened.

Oh, hang on a sec...

Jody just called us all over to her and announced that we're being split into three teams for the treasure hunt. I'm in her team with Isabella and Joelle. When she read out the teams, she gave me a secret wink, so I know she fixed it like that on purpose so that me and Isabella will have a chance to make up. I hope we do!

Thursday 8.41pm, waiting for my turn in the shower

I have volunteered to go last so I can write in here.

Guess what? Me and Bella have made up! And guess what else? Our team won the treasure hunt! Well, one special pony in particular won it, but I'll tell you about that in a minute.

Before we left the yard on the treasure hunt, Sally gave each team a map and their first clue. She explained that there would be three different sets of clues and three separate routes to follow, but that we would all meet up at the same final place to search for the treasure. Our team leaders had a cool saddle-bag each, packed with our sandwiches and water and the mobile and first-aid kit. Then Lydia handed out fluorescent bibs to wear over our riding clothes so we could easily be seen by any passing cars.

Sally said the only rule was that we had to stop for a half-hour lunch break so the ponies could have a rest. Our team went into the kitchen with Jody and worked out where the first clue was telling us to go, and then we got our ponies out and headed off.

Johnny's team had gone already but Sally's was still in the yard. We'd worked out that we needed to head for the church in the hamlet marked on the map.

We walked along the road for a little while and then turned up a track. It was good because we all talked together and even though Bella didn't say anything exactly to me she wasn't ignoring me either, and after a while I didn't feel so nervous around her. We trotted on and when we hit a nice wide uphill bit next to some fields we persuaded Jody to let us have a canter, to help us get ahead of the other teams. "Okay, then," she said, smiling. "Millie and her dad will be dragging their team across the countryside at high speed, so we might as well try to compete!"

Cantering up the hill was fantastic and I could tell that Cracker really loved being out of the manège!

It took about half an hour to get to the church and we found our next clue pinned to the noticeboard in the little stone porch. I dismounted and held Joelle's pony while she jumped down and ran to get it. It said:

Follow the green arrows.
Stick to the path.
Be good,
Or you'll end up like Little Red Riding Hood.

"Whoever wrote this isn't very good at poems!" I said, giggling. It was nice that Bella giggled at that too.

"Oh, thanks very much!" harrumphed Jody, but she was laughing.

"*You* wrote it!" I cried. "So you must know the answer!"

She nodded, but of course she wouldn't tell us where to go next or help us with the clue at all.

So we all dismounted and huddled round the map. After a while, Bella cried, "Aha! I've got it! Little Red Riding Hood was told to stick to the path through the woods in the fairy story, wasn't she?" She pointed at the woods marked on the map. "If we ride to the edge I bet we'll find that they've put some arrows up, maybe pinned to trees. Then we'll just have to follow them through the woods. As long as we stick to the path as the rhyme says we'll find our next clue."

"Well done, Bella, that's brilliant," I said.

"Thanks," she said, smiling, but she still didn't look exactly *at* me.

Jody said, "If that's what you girls think, then let's get going!"

"But are we right?" Bella asked. Jody just made a zipping her lips sign. She wasn't giving anything away!

"What do *you* think, Cracker?" I asked, and he actually whinnied right at that moment, making everyone laugh. "Cracker thinks you're right too," I told Bella. This time when she smiled, her eyes met mine and I started to think that things might turn out okay between us.

So we set off for the woods and sure enough there was a green arrow on a post where the

path entered them. We had to duck a bit under the trees at times and I was glad I'd put the bandages on Cracker, as there was a lot of bramble around.

After a few more green arrows, we came out
the other side on to a nice grassy bit by a field,
where we found a piece of paper pinned to a
tree. Our next clue!

Jody said we should have our lunch first
before working it out, and even though we
were keen to keep going, we were all pretty
hungry too. We dismounted, took off the
ponies' bridles and clipped our lead ropes to
their head collars – then the ponies could have
lunch too! Joelle needed the loo and Jody took
her back into the wood to go in private while
Bella and I held Bonny and Monsoon for them.
I knew it was my chance to talk to Bella – and I
took it.

It was really awkward at first and I didn't
know how to begin, but then suddenly I found
myself blurting it out. "I really *am* sorry I was
mean to you," I gabbled. "I did want Charm but
now I'm so glad I got Cracker and I'm just really,

really, *really* sorry and…" I trailed off then, not knowing what else to say. There was a horrible moment when I thought she was going to tell me to get lost and never speak to me again, but luckily she didn't. Instead she said, "That's okay, Chloe, I forgive you. And, well, you know why you got Cracker and not Charm, don't you?"

I shrugged. "Just the way things turned out, I suppose," I said.

"Chloe!" she cried. "Don't be dense! It's because Sally thinks you're a good rider. That's why she gave you a pony who needs more guidance."

I couldn't help but feel pleased. "Thanks," I said, "but maybe Sally thought I was a better rider than I am. I still can't get Cracker over that water jump. I'm going to have to wear a swimsuit in the comp tomorrow, because something tells me I'm going to get wet!"

Bella laughed at that and everything was okay

between us again, but we still shook hands to make it official. By the time Jody got back with Joelle, we were chatting away and she gave me a secret wink and looked really pleased.

We all sat down together and had our lunch, which was egg mayonnaise or ham rolls, and bananas for after – of course, Cracker managed to pinch half of mine! While we

were eating we worked out what the next clue meant and where we should go. The piece of paper said:

If you take the correct path,
The next clue you will find.
But don't go the wrong way,
Or you'll get left behind!

"That's not very helpful!" said Bella at first, glancing up the bridleway ahead of us, which forked into two paths. "It doesn't tell us which is the correct path. It's impossible!"

But I just grinned. I do crosswords with Mum all the time and they quite often say 'correct' to mean 'right', as in left and right. "It means take the right path, not the left," I explained. "'Correct' means 'right', and 'you'll get left behind' means if you take the left path you won't reach the treasure first. I'm pretty sure that's it."

"Chloe, you're a genius," said Bella, and I blushed with pride.

So we got back on our ponies and rode through the fields in walk, chatting. After ages of not finding the next clue, we got a bit worried we were falling behind the other teams, so we trotted on.

Luckily we soon found it, tacked to a fence post along the path. It said:

Up and down
And up again.
Not where fish fly,
But where birds swim.

Joelle got the giggles about that. "That's silly, birds don't swim!" she said.

"Ducks do," said Bella, smiling and pointing at the map.

There was a village with a duck pond marked on it about a mile away, and no sooner had she pointed it out than we were off. The path took us up a hill, then down a valley and up another hill, just as the clue said. We trotted as much as we could and had another canter when we came to a nice wide bit of path. Jody even let Bella and I jump a couple of low scrubby bushes, and it was so cool just doing it for fun and not worrying about knocked poles or clear rounds or anything. We got to the village quite quickly and saw Johnny's team, so we knew the treasure was nearby. On a post by the duck pond was our team's final clue. It said:

> Look for a red box,
> But don't rush
> Or you'll miss what's missing
> (In the . . . . . .)

We didn't know what the end bit meant, but we looked on the map and there was a red telephone box marked in the centre of the village. Bella and I started heading for it straight

away, but Jody called us back and made us calm
down and get in a line, us girls in front of her.
She said that there would be a few cars in the
village and we had to be sensible. So we were
careful, even though we could see Johnny's
team trotting on towards the phone box and all
I wanted to do was to break into a canter and
get there first. Then we saw Sally's team come
round the corner and trot towards the church,
so we knew they were on their second to last
clue, and would find the final one at the church
somewhere.

When we got to the phone
box, Mai was holding Twinkle
for Suki. I felt disappointed that
we'd lost, but then Suki came
out empty handed! "There's
nothing in there," she said.
"Sally's team must have
got here first."

But we told her that we'd seen them by the church, so they weren't even on this clue yet, and we were all really puzzled. Jody and Johnny just looked at each other, grinning. I knew by now they weren't going to give anything away even if we begged and pleaded. We all looked at the clue again. "It's warning us not to rush, but we all rushed to the phone box," said Mai. "Maybe we need to think again."

"How can you miss what's missing?" Bella wondered aloud.

I was confused for a moment too, but then I got it. "We mustn't miss that there's a word missing," I said. "It must be the end of the last line, because it doesn't make sense as it is. What rhymes with 'rush'?"

"Mush? Gush? Nothing!" cried Bella, getting frustrated.

I was busy trying to think of more things that rhymed with 'rush' but Cracker had other ideas.

He started wandering over to the hedge and I gathered up my reins and tried to steer him back to the group. "No, Cracker!" I told him. "Stop ignoring me! We're supposed to be a team, remember?"

But he just stuck his head in the hedge and when I finally managed to pull him up, he was chomping on a carrot! Well, it only took me about five seconds to realize that carrots don't grow on hedges, and I laughed out loud. "Over here!" I called out. "Cracker's found the treasure!"

I leaped down and pulled a red box out of the bush, as everyone trotted up to see. There was a carrot or apple for every pony in a tray on top of the

75

box and I had to quickly hand it up to Jody to stop Cracker from scoffing the lot!

"The missing word was 'bush!'" I told them.

"The phone box was a red herring – get it?" said Johnny.

"We would have got it sooner if the rhymes were better!" Mai replied, and we all giggled.

"Stop knocking the rhymes, they took me ages!" cried Jody, but she was laughing too.

"Well done, Cracker!" I said, giving him a big pat and a stroke. "You found the treasure. Clever boy!" He nuzzled my arm, so I knew he was happy too!

Sally's group caught up with us then and she asked who found the treasure. "Chloe did," said Bella, with a smile. I glanced nervously at Georgia, but she smiled at me too. She was obviously happy to forget about the falling out if

Bella was — what a relief!

"Actually, Cracker found it," I said.

"It sounds like a case of excellent teamwork to me," said Sally, and I just couldn't stop grinning.

Inside the red box were three cool pony notelet and envelope sets for the winning team. We let Joelle have first choice because she's the youngest, then I picked the one with the bay Welsh Section B on, because he looked a bit like Cracker — well, not the colour but the same cheeky eyes. There were mini chocolate bars in there too, one for everyone. We all got off to stretch our legs and ate them while feeding our ponies their prizes (except Cracker, of course, who'd already scoffed his. I made a big fuss of him though, in case he felt left out). Jody put our writing sets in her saddle-bag until we got back to the yard.

Then off we went, one long string of happy riders and ponies with no falling-outs.

When we got back and untacked, I had to give Cracker's carrotty bit a good scrub under the tap. But instead of thinking *urgh what a horrible job* it felt like one of my happiest moments ever — it was so fantastic just being on the yard in the sunshine with my friends, caring for my lovely pony. I wish I could stay here for ever and never go home!

Oh, the shower's free. Bye for now!

Very early on Friday morning!

I was going to write more last night but I fell asleep. I worked out that altogether we did two hours and twenty minutes of riding on the treasure hunt – no wonder I was tired out!

I woke up early, thinking about the jumping comp. Then I crept around getting dressed, but it still wasn't time to get up so I've got back into bed in my clothes!

Me and Bella shared out our notelets between the three of us so we all have the same, because we didn't want Georgia to feel left out. Then we had a fab idea – we're going to write thank yous to the Sunnyside staff for our brilliant week at Pony Camp. I can hardly bear to think that it's our last day, it's all just gone so fast! It's the jumping comp today – I can't believe it's come so quickly. Luckily we've got another lesson to work on it this morning. I just hope there's still time to turn things round with Cracker before the comp this afternoon. Dad's expecting to see me get a clear round and it will be awful if I get dumped in the water tray instead!

But whatever happens, I'm really looking forward to having a good time with my friends and my fab pony. I can't wait to fetch Cracker in from the field and get going.

Oh, cool, the alarm's just gone off. I know — I'll lie down and pretend to have just woken up, then Bella and Georgia will be amazed to see me in my clothes — ha ha!

Morning break on Friday

Hurrah! We finally made it over the water jump! My gorgeous Cracker is such a star!

After we'd warmed up, we went over all eight jumps at a lowish height, to get into the swing of things. Georgia got muddled up and she and Prince went the wrong way at first, and we all had poles down – so at least I didn't feel like the only one getting in a mess.

At first Cracker wouldn't go over the water jump, but I didn't get annoyed, because I could see everyone was having their own problems. And I knew he was trying – it wasn't his fault he didn't like the look of it.

After a few goes, with him running out every time, I was getting a bit downhearted. That's when Bella offered me a lead. Of course this time I said "yes please!". I followed a few paces behind Charm as we went round the corner and towards the water jump. Charm popped it easily, and Cracker just followed him over, almost before he realized what he was doing!

I gave him a big pat and thanked Bella loads. Sally told me to take him straight over again on my own and sure enough he jumped like a dream! I still had the gate down though, so no clear round yet. We'll just have to try really, really hard this afternoon and hope for the best.

Oh, gotta go, we're all going to tie our ponies up in the yard and make them look extra smart for the comp!

Just to quickly say...

...how gorgeous Cracker is looking! I've done some lovely little mane plaits, all I've got to do now is wind them up into neat knots. I've given his coat a really good brush and even put some bright blue ribbons in his tail. Now I've just got to get into my jodhs and sort my hair out and we're ready.

Oh, I've just looked out of the bedroom window and our car has pulled up. Mum and Dad are both getting out!

Friday night, snuggled up in my own bed!

Well, even though I'm not at Sunnyside Stables any more (boo!), I wanted to finish off my Pony Camp Diary by writing about what happened in the jumping comp.

It was so exciting riding into Group A's manège, which was set up as a practice area with just one jump in. We warmed up and had a couple of goes over the upright, then Sally explained that in the comp we would have two turns each, and as they wouldn't be timing us the aim was to get a clear round. We all wished each other luck, and then one by one we were called into the arena, where we had to bow to the judges (who were Lydia and Johnny).

Cracker and I started off okay. We were very close on the gate, but I couldn't look back to see whether it was down. I needed all my focus to get the turn right. We came through the middle of the arena and over the upright without a hitch, and I changed my canter lead. We approached the water jump straight and in a nice rhythm, but Cracker still ran out!

I was really disappointed because I thought we'd got that sorted out this morning, but I tried to keep calm and turned him round. We'd only had one refusal. We still had another chance. I was a bit nervous though and Cracker picked up on it, because he rushed at the jump, then swerved out again at the last minute. I managed to stay on but I felt my heart sink – we hadn't gone clear. We weren't alone though – no one had managed a clear round except for Georgia.

After I dismounted I stood fiddling with Cracker's girth for no reason, to avoid having to go over to my parents. When I saw Dad coming towards me, I was going to pretend I had something urgent to do in the tack room. But in the end I stayed put because I didn't want to miss any of my time with Cracker.

As Dad reached us, I stiffened and Cracker gave me an inquisitive look and nuzzled my arm. He could tell something was wrong. I looked up at Dad and decided to get the first word in. "Okay, so I didn't get a clear round, but so what? It's really hard, you know," I mumbled.

But instead of being cross, Dad just held his hands in the air. "Chloe, calm down!" he cried. "I think you're doing really well and so does Mum."

"But I promised I'd get a clear round, that's why you came..." I began.

"It's you who kept talking about getting a clear round," said Dad, "not me. Honestly, I just want you to enjoy yourself. We all think you're doing brilliantly."

"Really?" I mumbled.

Dad put his arm round my shoulder. "Maybe I don't say it often enough, but I'm so proud of you, Chloe," he said. I looked up at him and his eyes were twinkling. I could tell he really meant it.

Sally called over to us that it was time to begin round two and I got Dad to hold my other stirrup while I remounted.

"Good luck, we'll be rooting for you," he said, with a big smile on his face.

I looked over at Mum, who waved and gave me a thumbs up.

Georgia went first this time, and she had that horrid spread down, but at least she'd gone clear in the first round, so she didn't mind too much.

Bella got a clear and I expected a little bit of my old jealousy to come back, but none did. I just felt really happy for her and Charm. Millie looked very determined in this round and we were all cheering for her, but Tally picked up too much speed on the first corner, did a handbrake turn to the bounce and ended up jumping quite long and knocking the second pole. We all gave them a big clap, though, for a good try. Millie didn't look remotely bothered about not going clear. But she's lucky, she'll probably get another chance next week!

Then it was my turn.

Everyone was cheering and clapping as I rode by, but when I got into the arena I didn't hear a thing. All there was in the world were me and Cracker and the jumps. I remembered to look up and ahead and concentrate on where we were going this time, and I just let Cracker get on with jumping.

We started off a bit messy over the cross pole and spread, but everything stayed up (phew!) and we got into a good rhythm round the nice wide arc at the top of the arena, which set us up much better for the bounce and brush. We got over the middle jump without a hitch but I only let myself be pleased for a split

second, then refocussed and asked Cracker to
trot to change our canter lead. Then we were
off round the tight bend and over the dreaded
gate. This time Cracker seemed to know it
was a danger zone and did a huge leap over,
more than clearing it. He started getting really
excited after that, but I kept him nice and steady
round the bend and over the upright. Then we
were setting ourselves up for the water jump.
I consciously breathed out and sank into the
saddle. I had to let Cracker know I was relaxed,
and then he would be too. I looked up and
ahead at the finish, as if the jump wasn't even
there, and before I knew it we were over!

We'd done it — a clear round!
Mum and Dad were
cheering like crazy and I rode
out of the arena grinning
from ear to ear.
In the practice area

I leaped off and made a huge fuss of Cracker – what a total star pony! And what a fab team we'd made!

All us Group B girls said a big well done to each other and as I was walking Cracker back into the yard, my parents came up to meet me. Mum gave me a hug and Dad said, "Well done, Chloe, that was excellent."

When we'd put our ponies back in their stables for a rest, us Group B girls got our drinks and biscuits from the kitchen, then we all sat at the edge of the other manège together to watch the younger girls play some gymkhana games. It was great fun and we cheered wildly for all of them.

Then later there was a prize-giving and we brought our ponies out again and collected our rosettes. I felt so proud of the clear round. And I felt even prouder that me and Cracker did it as a team – together.

I tied the rosette on to his bridle and Dad took some pictures of our group and our ponies all together, and then we asked Lydia to take one of my whole family with Cracker in the middle. Cracker nuzzled Mum's arm and she looked a bit nervous in case he nibbled her sleeve!

When it was all over, I led Cracker to the barn. I gave him a carrot I'd scrounged from Jody and spent ages fussing and stroking him while I brushed him down.

I felt upset about leaving him, but I'm planning to go back next year – I'm already trying to persuade Mum to book it!

It was really sad saying goodbye to Bella and Georgia. Dad took loads of photos of us three though, and I'm going to send some to them tomorrow, with my first letter. We've all promised to write to each other using the pony paper and envelopes!

Just as we were heading to the car with all our bags we remembered the thank-you letters we'd written, which were in my bag. I heaped all my stuff on to Dad and ran back over to the yard. Sally was there in the office so I gave her the letters.

As she opened hers, her face lit up. "Oh, thanks so much, Chloe, that's very kind of you!" she said. "Thank the other girls for me, won't you?"

I nodded and made for the door. "Chloe," she said then, and I whirled round in the doorway. "You've really turned it around this week," she told me. "I'm so proud of you, well done."

I couldn't help beaming. "Thanks, but it was all down to Cracker!" I said, and I skipped out and across the yard.

I really learnt a lot at Pony Camp, and not just about jumping! I've made some wonderful new friends, met some fab ponies and found out what a true partnership is — all thanks to Cracker!

Hey, I've just realized that Sally was right — when she warned me not to be so desperate to achieve my goals that it actually stopped me succeeding I didn't really understand what she meant. But I do now. As soon as I started to relax and work as a team with Cracker, we did so much better — and I had a lot more fun, too! How funny that nearly all week I thought I had to teach *him*, but actually he's taught *me* loads!

Now, I wonder which pony I'll get next year?!

PONY CAMP
diaries

Learn all about
the world of ponies!

☙ Glossary ❧

Bending – directing the horse to ride correctly around a curve.

Bit – the piece of metal that goes inside the horse's mouth. Part of the bridle.

Chase Me Charlie – a show jumping game where the jumps get higher and higher.

Currycomb – a comb with rows of metal teeth used to clean (to curry) a pony's coat.

Dandy brush – a brush with hard bristles that removes the dirt, hair, and any other debris stirred up by the currycomb.

Frog – the triangular soft part on the underside of the horse's hoof. It's very important to clean around it with a hoof pick.

Girth – the band attached to the saddle and buckled around the horse's barrel to keep the saddle in place.

Grooming – the daily cleaning and caring for the horse to keep it healthy and make it beautiful for competitions. A full groom includes brushing its coat, mane and tail and picking out the hooves.

Gymkhana – a fun event full of races and other competitions.

Hands – a way to measure the height of a horse.

Glossary

Mane – the long hair on the back of a horse's neck. Perfect for plaiting!

Manège – an enclosed training area for horses and their riders.

Numnah – a piece of material that lies under the saddle and stops it from rubbing against the horse's back.

Paces – a horse has four main paces, each made up of an evenly repeated sequence of steps. From slowest to quickest, these are the walk, trot, canter and gallop.

Plodder – a slow, reliable horse.

Pommel – the raised part at the front of the saddle.

Pony – a horse under 14.2 hands in height.

Rosette – a rose-shaped decoration with ribbons awarded as a prize! Usually, a certain colour matches the place you come in during the competition.

Stirrups – foot supports attached to the sides of a horse's saddle.

Tack – the main pieces of the horse's equipment, including the saddle and bridle. Tacking up a horse means getting it ready for riding.

৵ Pony Colours ৵

*Ponies come in all kinds of **colours**. These are some of the most common!*

Bay – Bay ponies have rich brown bodies and black manes, tails and legs.

Black – A true black pony will have no brown hairs and the black can be so pure that it looks a bit blue!

Chestnut – Chestnut ponies have reddish-brown coats that vary from light to dark red with no black points.

Dun – A dun pony has a sandy-coloured body, with a black mane, tail and legs.

Grey – Grey ponies come in a range of colour varieties, including dapple grey, steel grey, and rose grey.

Palomino – Palominos have a sandy-coloured body with a white or cream mane and tail. Their coats can range from pale yellow to bright gold!

Piebald – Piebald ponies have a mixture of black patches and white patches – like a cow!

Skewbald – Skewbald ponies have patches of white and brown.

Pony Markings

*As well as the main body colour, many ponies also have white **markings** on their faces and legs!*

On the legs:

Socks – run up above the fetlock but lower than the knee. The fetlock is the joint above the hoof.

Stockings – extend to at least the bottom of the horse's knee, sometimes higher.

On the face:

Blaze – a wide, straight stripe down the face from in between the eyes to the muzzle.

Snip – a white marking on the horse's muzzle, between the nostrils.

Star – a white marking between the eyes.

Stripe – the same as a blaze but narrower.

White/bald face – a very wide blaze that goes out past the eyes, making most of the horse's face look white!

Fan-tack-stic Cleaning Tips!

*Get your **tack** shining in no time with these top tips!*

- Clean your tack after every use, if you can. Otherwise, make sure you at least rinse the bit under running water and wash off any mud or sweat from your girth after each ride.
- The main things you will need are:
  - bars of saddle soap
  - a soft cloth
  - a sponge
  - a bottle of leather conditioner
- As you clean your bit, check that it has no sharp edges and isn't too worn.
- Use a bridle hook or saddle horse to hold your bridle and saddle as you clean them. If you don't have a saddle horse, you can hang a blanket over a gate. Avoid hanging your bridle on a single hook or nail because the leather might crack!

- Make sure you look carefully at the bridle before undoing it so that you know how to put it back together!
- Use the conditioner to polish the leather of the bridle and saddle and make them sparkle!
- Check under your numnah before you clean it. If the dirt isn't evenly spread on both sides, you might not be sitting evenly as you ride.
- Polish your metalwork occasionally. Cover the leather parts around it with a cloth and only polish the rings – not the mouthpiece, because that would taste horrible!

꧁ Jumping Time! ꧂

Find out how much you know about show jumping with this fun quiz!

1. Which of these types of jump does not exist in show jumping competitions?
    a. Hoop
    b. Skinny
    c. Table

2. How many faults is a "knockdown" worth?
    a. None
    b. Two
    c. Four

3. How many refusals is your pony allowed before elimination?
    a. One
    b. Two
    c. Three

4. How many faults do you get for falling off your pony?
    a. Four
    b. Six
    c. Three

5. Which of these pony events does not include jumping?

   a. Dressage
   b. Cross-country
   c. Hunt seat

6. What position would you and your pony have finished in if you won a red rosette?

   a. First place
   b. Second place
   c. Third place

7. In which year was the first show jumping competition held in the U.K.?

   a. 1910
   b. 1907
   c. 1915

8. What is an "oxer"?

   a. A type of bit
   b. A special blanket for the pony
   c. A wide jump

Pretty Plaits!

Follow this step-by-step guide to give your pony a perfect tail plait!

1. Start at the very top of the tail and take two thin bunches of hair from either side, plaiting them into a strand in the centre.

2. Continue to pull in bunches from either side and plait down the centre of the tail.

3. Keep plaiting like this, making sure you're pulling the hair tightly to keep the plait from unravelling!

4. When you reach the end of the dock – where the bone ends – stop taking in bunches from the side but keep plaiting downwards until you run out of hair.

5. Fasten with a plait band!

Gymkhana Ready!

Get your pony looking spectacular for the gymkhana with these grooming ideas!

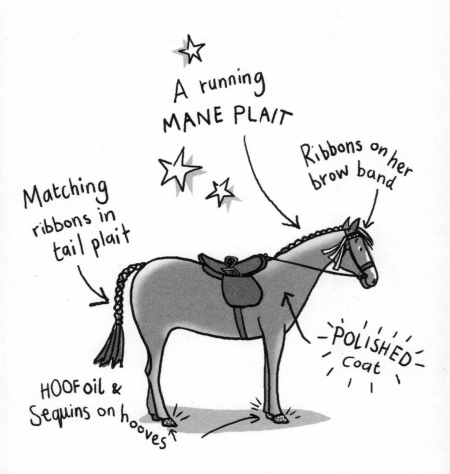

A running
MANE PLAIT

Ribbons on her
brow band

Matching
ribbons in
tail plait

POLISHED
Coat

HOOF oil &
Sequins on hooves↑

Turn the page for a sneak peek
at the next story in the series!

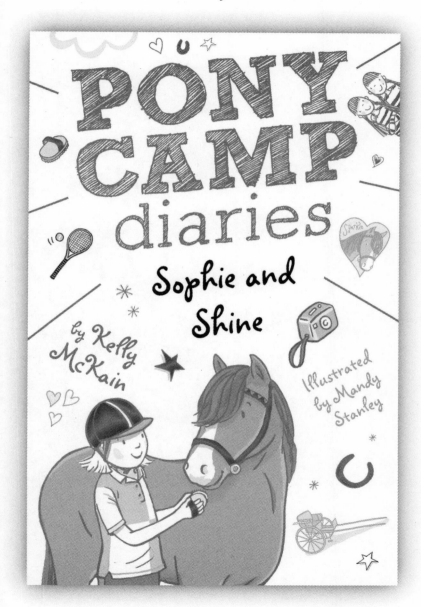

PONY CAMP
diaries

Sophie and
Shine

by Kelly
McKain

Illustrated
by Mandy
Stanley

Monday afternoon
—I'm at Pony Camp!

We've just had lunch on my very first day at Pony Camp, and I thought I'd start writing in my fab new diary straight away. Jody, who runs Sunnyside Stables, gave us one each to write all our adventures in while we're here and I've had such an exciting time already! We had our assessment lesson this morning and I've been given the best pony ever. She's called Shine and she's absolutely gorgeous! I'll write more about her in a minute but I'm going to start right at the beginning so I don't miss anything out.

We were a bit late arriving because my baby brother Albie was screaming and Dad couldn't get him strapped into the car seat. Plus, Mum had to pack all his stuff, like his bottles and nappies and pushchair, and even with me helping it took ages.

Albie needs as much for one car journey as I do for a week!

So by the time we got here everyone else was already unpacked and on the yard. Jody showed me upstairs and I had to quickly dump my stuff in the room where I'm staying. I took the top bunk, as someone's towel and nightie were already on the bottom one. There was also an unmade bed by the window covered in soft toy ponies, and Jody told me it belonged to her daughter, Millie.

Jody

Millie

Sally

I hurried down to the yard and Sally the head instructor gave us a welcome talk, and introduced all the yard staff. Then Jody told us

about bedtimes and meals and stuff, and said
to come to her if we had any problems or
questions. Jody's really nice and though she's
Millie's actual mum, she's going to be like a mum
to all of us while we're staying here.

Then Sally got us to introduce ourselves to
each other and I found out that
the other girl (on the bunk below
me) is called Beth. She's my age but
a bit smaller than me, and she's got
lovely wavy hair (I'm always trying to
get mine to go like that but it never
does!). She looked a bit nervous and
asked me if I'd done much riding before.

I explained that while I've been riding for
quite a few years, I don't get to go very often
any more because of Mum and Dad being so
busy with Albie. "So I've done lots of flatwork
and some jumping but I've probably forgotten
loads of it," I told her. "Actually, that's one of

the things I'm most looking forward to on this holiday – working on my riding non-stop for a whole week!" Then I suddenly panicked thinking what if Millie and Beth are really good, but Beth said, "I've done way less than you – I only started a few months ago, when me and Dad moved down here."

We both turned to Millie at the exact same time and said, "I bet you're brilliant," which was so spooky it made all three of us collapse into giggles. Millie said, "I've been riding a long time, but if I can get my pony to do what I want it's a miracle." Her pony's called Tally and she says his main hobby is bombing off on hacks and dragging her through hedges.

The other girls are lovely too, and I especially like Shanice. She's really smiley and said she

liked my new black cord jodhs (I had to get new ones because when I tried on my riding stuff last week I'd grown out of my old ones!). Shanice lives in London and she's hardly ridden at all, but she's so pony mad she saved up for a really nice grooming kit to use on her pony this week. She got given a cute piebald called Prince and she fell in love with him straight away.

The three older girls are really cool. Aneela has amazingly long shiny hair and Izzy's got a fab purple silk she bought specially for this week. Courtney's wearing make-up and when I said I liked her eyeshadow she offered to do a makeover on me one night! Her mum's actually a

beauty therapist so Courtney's learnt all about
make-up and hair and face packs and stuff from
her. Who haven't I mentioned yet? Oh, yes,

Daisy and Grace are the youngest,
they're identical twins and even
their riding gear is exactly the
same (I don't know how we'll
ever tell them apart!).

After a quick tour round
the yard, we were all given our
ponies. It was so exciting waiting
to hear who I'd got. Sally read our names off a
list as Lydia brought the ponies out one by one,
and that's when I met my gorgeous Shine! Lydia
had tacked up the ponies for us this once but
we'll be doing that ourselves for the rest of the
week. It's so great that we get to do everything
for them as well as all the riding. It's almost like
actually owning one. I used to ask and ask and
ask Mum and Dad if I could have my own pony,

but they kept saying no, so I stopped eventually. But it's still my number one dream and I secretly think about it a lot and imagine what it would be like.

Shine's exactly the sort of pony I've been dreaming about! She's a really pretty bay and so sweet and friendly. At 13.2hh she's the perfect size for me too! She's got a beautiful glossy coat and I'm going to make it gleam for the gymkhana on Friday. I feel so lucky that I got her!

I've brought my digital camera and I've taken pix of everyone and their ponies, but there's nowhere here to print them off, so instead I'll have to do some drawings of us all. I know, I'll make it into a puzzle.

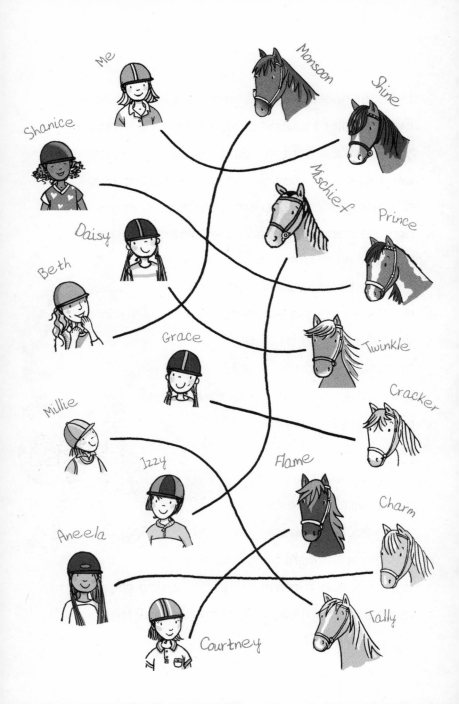

As we were given our ponies, we led them over to the mounting block and got on, ready for the assessment lesson. I had to walk Shine away from the crowd a bit before sorting out my stirrups. She wasn't that keen on standing right near the others and she kept on swishing her tail and shifting about.

It felt strange being back on a pony at first, but in the assessment lesson we had a good long walk round on each rein, so I had time to think about my position and get used to Shine. We did lots of halts, circles and changes of direction to get our ponies listening to us. It took me a while to remember to look around to see where I was going, though! Shine is quite forward-going in trot so I could go rising in a nice rhythm without nagging her all the time. Sally called out to me to change my trot diagonal, though, and I realized I'd forgotten to even check it!

When we had a canter I slid my outside leg back and Shine did as I asked straight away. I'd forgotten how fast it felt – but also how fun! Sally had to tell me to sit back and down, and stop clinging to the reins, but I didn't really mind her saying that because she calls things out to everyone. Shanice hasn't cantered before so she had a trot instead, and Sally said she'd be cantering by the end of the week, no worries. It's great that things are coming back to me already – and it helps that Shine's so lovely to ride! It was just so exciting – and to think, I've got loads more canters to go before the end of the week!

Afterwards we untacked (I helped Shanice with Prince as she hadn't done it before), and then we all gathered back on the yard to hear what groups we'd be in. Sally said I was borderline but she's putting me in Group A to start off with (the beginners' group) so I can find my feet and brush up my skills. If I do well she's going to move me up to Group B. I'm really disappointed to be honest, and can't help thinking that if Mum and Dad hadn't been so busy with Albie. . . Still, I suppose moving groups can be a goal for me to work towards.

We then had a lecture about safety on the yard and Lydia showed us where everything was and how to put things away properly so nothing got tripped over or lost. It was fun because she pretended to do dangerous things like mounting without her chin strap done up, or tying up a pony without using a slip-knot, and we had to stop her by calling out "No!" and saying what was wrong.

Then at lunch Aneela was doing impressions

of a teacher at her riding school at home who has this really snooty voice and we were all in stitches. She's so funny — in fact, all the girls here are nice. We've just been trying on each others' stuff. Daisy's blue fleece really suited Shanice and Izzy's purple silk looked great on Courtney's hat, and she said she really wishes she'd bought a new one before she came, too. Grace insisted on trying on Aneela's jodhs and of course they were miles too long for her! I know I'm going to have a fab week with them all!

Jody just gave us our welcome letters (I've stuck mine in the front of this diary) and we found out we're going carriage-driving this week — we're all really excited. It'll be great fun going on a trip together and only Izzy has been in a carriage before, when she was a bridesmaid at her cousin's wedding, so it'll be a brand new

COURTNEY wearing IZZY'S silk

horsey experience too!

We've got to go back on the yard again now for our first Pony Care lecture – it's on tack and tacking up. I'm going to pay extra special attention in the lectures because maybe if I show Mum and Dad how much I've learnt they'll understand how serious I am about getting my own pony, and then they might start to think about it at least.

Also available…

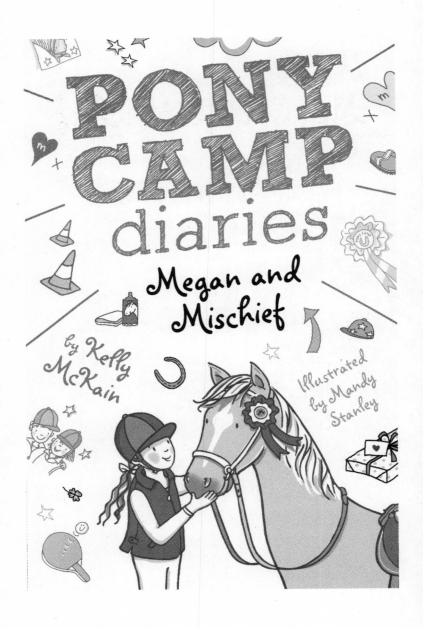

PONY CAMP diaries

Megan and Mischief

by Kelly McKain

Illustrated by Mandy Stanley

Megan and Mischief

I'm so excited to be here
at Pony Camp!

I can't wait to meet my pony,
but I'm a little nervous, too,
because I've asked for a
really fast one. I'm ready
to be Megan the Brave -
hopefully I can rise
to the challenge!

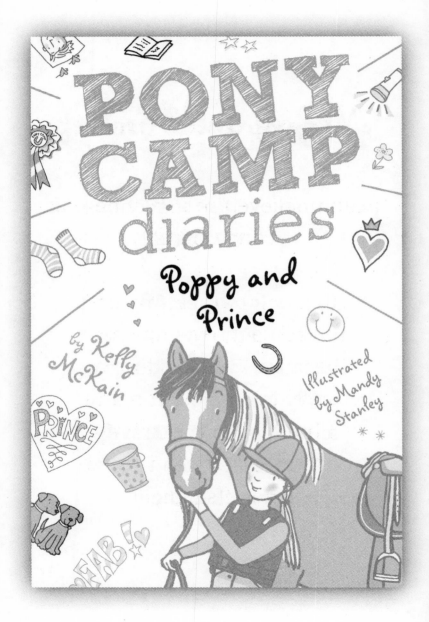

PONY CAMP
diaries

Poppy and Prince

by Kelly McKain

Illustrated by Mandy Stanley

PRINCE

FAB!

Poppy and Prince

I can't believe I'm finally here at
Pony Camp!

The only thing is, I haven't
ridden a pony since my
big fall at a show jumping
competition last month.
I hope I can control my
nerves and get back
in the saddle!

Kelly McKain

Kelly McKain is a best-selling children's and YA author with more than 40 books published in more than 20 languages. She lives in the beautiful Surrey Heath area with her family and loves horses, dancing, yoga, singing, walking, and being in nature. She came up with the idea for the Pony Camp Diaries while she was helping young riders at a summer camp, just like the one at Sunnyside Stables! She enjoys hanging out at the Holistic Horse and Pony Centre, where she plays with and rides cute Smartie and practices her natural horsemanship skills with the Quantum Savvy group. Her dream is to do some bareback, bridleless jumping like New Zealand Free Riding ace Alycia Burton, but she has a ways to go yet!